Disney

sonny

WITH A CHANCE

making the Cut

Adapted by N. B. Grace

Based on the series created by Steve Marmel

Part One is based on the episode, "Promises, Prom-misses," Written by Dava Savel

Part Two is based on the episode, "You've Got Fan Mail," Written by Phil Baker & Drew Vaupen

DISNEP PRESS
New York

Printed in the United States of America

First Edition
1 3 5 7 9 10 8 6 4 2
J689-1817-1-09305

Library of Congress Control Number on file.
ISBN 978-1-4231-2276-0

For more Disney Press fun, visit www.disneybooks.com
Visit DisneyChannel.com

PART
ONE

CHAPTER 1

Sonny Munroe had just headed off the set of *So Random!*, the popular sketch-comedy show that she was currently starring in. She was so busy looking down at her phone that she didn't see where she was going. "I can't believe I missed it," she said to herself with a sigh.

"Whoa, watch it!" a voice suddenly yelled out.

Sonny looked up in surprise to see Chad Dylan Cooper, the supercute star of *Mackenzie*

Falls, a romantic teen drama that filmed nearby. Even though she had a little bit of a crush on him, she would never admit it to anyone. And he was way too arrogant for Sonny to ever really take him seriously.

"I'm so sorry," Sonny began to say. Then she noticed that Chad had a huge bruise on his face. "Oh, my gosh!" she exclaimed. "What happened?"

"I just got in a huge fight over at *Mackenzie Falls*," Chad said nonchalantly. "We were shooting a scene. I know, it's hard to believe I could look this good when I look this bad, huh?" he said, pushing his blond hair out of his eyes. "What's up with you?"

"Nothing," Sonny said, a hint of disappointment in her voice. "I missed my prom back home, and I just got some pictures from my best friend, so . . ." she told him, her voice trailing off.

Chad shrugged. "You're not missing much. I've been to a bunch of proms, and they've all ended in disaster," he told Sonny.

"Oh, I'm sorry to hear that," Sonny said sympathetically.

"Yeah, episode ten, my hair caught on fire. Last year's season finale, my date turned out to be my long-lost sister," Chad stated, shaking his head.

Sonny looked at him in confusion. "What?" she asked. "Uh, Chad, those are fake proms."

Chad rolled his eyes. "Fake proms, real proms, they all stink."

"No, they don't!" Sonny exclaimed. "They're romantic! You know, a girl dreams her whole life about going to the prom and having that perfect dance with a very special guy," she said dreamily.

Chad yawned. "Then he gets hit on the head by a faulty disco ball. Episode sixteen," he said.

Sonny couldn't believe what she was hearing. Even though she was pretty new to the West Coast, having just recently moved from a small town in Wisconsin, she couldn't believe that Chad wasn't the tiniest bit interested in going to a prom. These Hollywood types were proving to be too much!

"You know what, Chad?" she told him. "You wouldn't know a real romance if it punched you in the face. In fact, you wouldn't know a real *punch* in the face if it punched you in the face, because there's nothing real about you!" she shouted.

Chad's eyes narrowed. "Oh, well, here's something real for you. I really don't want to stand here and talk to you!" he retorted.

"Good!" Sonny shot back. "Because I really don't want to stand here and talk to you!" And with that, she stomped away.

CHAPTER 2

A few minutes later, Sonny was on her way to the prop house near the set of *So Random!* The prop house was a favorite hangout for the cast members. It was filled with lots of cool props from the set, and a relaxing spot for the group, especially after a live performance. Sonny was dying to tell someone about what had just happened with Chad, and hoped some of the cast would be there.

Sure enough, when Sonny arrived, they were all there. Sonny spotted Tawni Hart, the self-proclaimed star of the show, along with Grady Mitchell and Nico Harris—two of the funniest guys Sonny had ever met. Zora Lancaster was there, too. She was the youngest member of the cast, and was known to be a bit of a prankster on the set. Each member of the cast was pretty different, and that's what made *So Random!* work so well. Each person brought their own uniqueness to the show.

Sonny began to tell Tawni what had happened with Chad. "Well, he said that all proms stink," Sonny explained. "They *don't* stink! You guys know that." She paused, waiting for her castmates to nod in agreement. But all four of them just looked at her sheepishly. "Oh, my gosh, you *don't* know that," she realized. "You've never been to a prom, have you?" She gave the group a serious look.

"I've been working since my first diaper commercial!" Tawni said defensively.

"I'm eleven," Zora replied.

"I was on the road, doing my one-man show," Nico added.

Sonny couldn't believe it. But then she suddenly had an idea. She grinned at her castmates. "Well, we're going to change all that because I'm thinking we can have our own prom!" she exclaimed.

Grady looked confused. "You mean a prom *sketch*?"

Sonny shook her head. "No, like a *real* prom," she told them. "With dancing and twinkly lights and a really cool theme!" She looked at her castmates expectantly.

Nico raised his hand to suggest a theme. "Girls," he said, grinning flirtatiously. Nico liked to think of himself as something of a ladies' man. The reality was quite a bit different, but Sonny didn't want to burst his bubble. Instead, she gave him a cautionary look. "That's not a theme, Nico."

Nico just shrugged. It was worth a try.

Sonny continued. "I'm thinking we should have a really cool theme. You know, something fantastic, something magical, something we've all dreamed about," she said wistfully.

"Tawni Town!" Tawni shouted.

Sonny gave her an exasperated look. Couldn't she take this just a *little* bit more seriously?

"What?" Tawni asked innocently. "It's a great dream!"

"I was thinking about something a little more romantic, like 'A Night in the Clouds,'" Sonny told the group. She had a faraway look in her eyes.

Grady raised his hand. "You know what?" he said. "I'm on board. I'll do music." To demonstrate his DJ skills, he pretended to scratch an album. "Wickie, wickie, wickie," he joked.

Nico frowned at Grady. "Dude, if you do music, you won't be able to dance with any cute girls," he pointed out.

10

Grady shrugged. "I don't know how to dance," he replied.

"Well, it's time you enrolled at the Nico School of Dance," Nico told him. He prided himself on his dancing skills.

"But I just promised her I'd do music," Grady responded.

"First lesson is free," Nico told him.

"Sonny, first lesson is *free!*" Grady exclaimed, turning to Sonny. He was definitely into the idea of getting some dance lessons from Nico, who was always a big hit on the dance floor.

Sonny laughed. "Fine, I'll do 'wickie, wickie, wickie,'" she said, imitating what Grady had done earlier. "Okay, who's going to do food?" she asked. She looked around the group hopefully. Not one person volunteered.

"Fine," she said, sighing. "I'll do food. Invites?"

Nico raised his hand and smiled. Sonny beamed at him, trying to convince him.

"Thank you, Nico," Sonny said gratefully. Finally, someone was getting into the prom spirit!

"Oh, I was going to suggest you do that, too," he said.

"You know what?" Sonny said. "I'm happy to do everything. I want this prom to be *perfect*."

"Then I accept," Tawni suddenly chimed in.

"What?" Sonny asked.

"I will be prom queen," she replied. "Now stop begging!"

Sonny hesitated. She knew—as did everyone else—that Tawni *loved* the spotlight. She loved it so much, in fact, that she couldn't stand it when anyone else got even a tiny bit of attention.

But Sonny couldn't bring herself to guarantee Tawni the prom-queen spot. After all, the prom queen was traditionally voted on by the student body of the school, or in this case, the cast and crew of *So Random!* But Sonny remained quiet, for now.

Suddenly, Zora spoke up. "Are we bringing dates to this shindig?" she asked. "Because I just broke up with my boyfriend, Holloway."

Nico's jaw dropped in disbelief. The girl who liked to hide in the ceiling vent to eavesdrop and play pranks on people had been *dating* someone?

"You had a boyfriend named Holloway?" Nico asked.

Zora shrugged. "Yeah," she said casually. "Why don't you put me in charge of security?" she asked Sonny, changing the subject.

Sonny made a note on her clipboard. "Why don't we make this a no-date, no-*drama* prom," she suggested. Then she thought for a moment. "But we *should* invite kids from the other TV shows around the lot. Who's with me?" she asked eagerly.

"I am!" Grady exclaimed.

"That sounds good," Nico said in agreement, nodding his head.

"I'm with that," Zora chimed in.

"Well, as long as you're doing everything, why not?" Tawni replied.

"That's the spirit!" Sonny cheered. The group looked at each other and smiled.

The first *So Random!* prom was under way!

CHAPTER 3

Full of confidence, Sonny headed for Marshall Pike's office. She just knew the show's producer would love her idea. Or, at least, she really hoped he would. When she arrived, he was standing behind his desk, toying with his brand-new GPS device.

"Please proceed south for point zero six miles," the recorded voice on the GPS said.

Marshall obediently took a few steps forward—and bumped right into his desk.

"Ow!" he yelped.

Sonny walked into the office just in time to hear him cry out in pain. "Is this a bad time?" she asked.

Marshall frowned at the device. "Stupid GPS," he muttered. "I can't figure out how it works. I've been trying to get to the bathroom for the last thirty minutes."

Sonny raised an eyebrow. "It's down the hall, where it's always been," she pointed out.

"*I* know that," the producer huffed. "And *you* know that." He held up his GPS device. "But *it* doesn't know that!" He sighed and tried to put his technological problems behind him. "What can I do for you?"

Sonny gave him a cheerful smile. "Marshall, I just wanted to let you know that we're going to have a prom," she told him.

"Thanks for the heads-up," he replied. "But no."

"What?" Sonny asked. "Oh, I know. I forgot to say the magic words," she joked. "Please, may I?"

"No," Marshall repeated.

Sonny tried another tactic. "Maybe if you knew the theme?" she asked hopefully.

Marshall gave her a curious look. "What is it?" he asked slowly.

Sonny smiled. " 'A Night in the Clouds,' " she announced proudly.

"Oh, that's nice!" Marshall exclaimed. "But no." He wasn't giving into her idea—at all.

Sonny frowned. "What do you have against proms?" she asked, disappointed.

The producer gave her a sympathetic look. "Look, I have nothing against proms," he began. "But if I let you have a prom, I have to give in to everybody. Nico gets his carnival, Grady gets his puppet show, and we'll all be living in Tawni Town. Is that what you want? Do you *really* want to be living in Tawni Town?" he asked, giving Sonny a serious look.

"I hear it's a heck of a town," Sonny replied with a laugh. She was really hoping Marshall would change his mind. But he wasn't budging.

Sonny sighed. "I'll take that as a no," she said. She couldn't believe it. Was she never going to get to go to a prom?

Back in the prop house, Nico was giving Grady a dance lesson. Grady was dancing with a mannequin, while Tawni and Zora were watching his awkward movements. They were trying not to laugh.

"You're very light on your feet, my dear," Grady joked to his dancing partner. "I think we make quite the couple."

"First lesson's going well," Nico said encouragingly. "Now dip!"

Grady dipped the mannequin. Unfortunately, his dip was *very* enthusiastic. So enthusiastic, in fact, that the mannequin's head fell right off and rolled onto the floor.

He looked up at Nico, shocked. "That's not *actually* going to happen, is it?"

Before Nico could reply, Sonny walked into the room. Her castmates looked at her, eager to find out what Marshall had said.

Sonny shook her head. "Prom's off, everybody," she said sadly.

Tawni's eyes widened with shock. "But I've been dreaming about being prom queen since you brought it up eighteen minutes ago!"

"I'm sorry. I tried," Sonny said. "I even used the magic word."

"This is like the puppet show all over again!" Grady complained.

"Guys, no one is more disappointed than I am," Sonny responded.

"You *had* to ask Marshall," Nico said disapprovingly.

Zora looked over at Sonny and shook her head. "Always got to do everything by the book," she added.

Sonny looked at the group defensively. "Oh, yeah?" she scoffed. "Is that what you think? Is that what you *all* think?"

Tawni gave Sonny an exasperated look. "Yeah, that's what we think," she said, tossing her hair over to one side. "That's what you do."

"Well, I just checked out a new book," Sonny said defiantly. "And it's called, *'We're Having a Secret Prom,'* by Sonny Munroe."

Her friends stared at each other. What could Sonny mean?

"Are you suggesting—" Nico began.

Sonny nodded. "That's right," she said. "A *'secret* prom.'"

Tawni got a wistful look in her eyes. "A 'secret prom,'" she repeated in a hushed voice.

"A 'secret prom,'" Zora said gleefully.

"A 'secret prom,'" Nico repeated, as if thinking it over.

Sonny held up her hand. "Okay, I think we've said it enough times," she said quickly. "We're having a '*secret* prom.'"

Grady raised an eyebrow. "How come *you* get to say it again?" he demanded.

Sonny lifted her chin proudly. "Because I wrote the book," she answered with a smile.

CHAPTER 4

The next day, Nico and Grady were back on the set. They ran down the hall, carrying a tall ladder. Just as they passed Marshall's door, he stepped out of his office. Luckily for them, he was holding his GPS device and didn't notice what they were doing. He started to take a step forward, but the GPS automated voice said, "Please continue to hold, while I recalculate your route."

Marshall sighed with exasperation. This gadget was proving to be more trouble than it was worth!

Then Zora and Tawni sneaked down into the hallway as soon as Marshall was safely out of sight. Zora was holding a punch bowl and Tawni was carrying an armful of clothing. Sonny emerged from one of the offices clutching a sparkly disco ball. As she stealthily crept down the hall, she ran right into who else but Chad Dylan Cooper! As happy as Sonny might have been to see him, she didn't have the time to stop and chat.

"Hey, Sonny!" he said cheerfully. As usual, he looked . . . well, perfect. His blond hair was slightly tousled, and his outfit was casual but hip.

"Hey, Chad, can't talk, I'm in a hurry," Sonny said quickly.

"Oh, right . . . right," Chad said. "The 'secret prom.'" He smirked at her. "Not much of a 'secret' when every kid in the lot's walking around with fliers that read"—he whispered sarcastically—"'*secret prom.*'" He held up one of her posters.

It read, WINTER WONDERLAND. SHH! IT'S A SECRET!

"Aren't you excited?" Sonny asked, smiling. "I am *so* excited. I'm even excited about how excited I am," she continued, unable to contain her enthusiasm.

"We're not feeling that over at *Mackenzie Falls*," Chad said in a bored tone. "Mostly they're saying it's dumb."

The cheerful look on Sonny's face suddenly disappeared. "Maybe you and your little snobby friends at *Mackenzie Falls* shouldn't come," she told him.

Chad looked at her and shrugged. "Maybe we won't," he replied.

Sonny put a hand on her hip. "Good, because you're officially *uninvited*." She couldn't believe how much nerve he had!

Chad glared at her. "Good," he retorted. "Because we wouldn't have come anyway." He gave her an icy stare.

"You're only saying that because I just uninvited you," Sonny replied, glaring back at him.

"You're only uninviting me because I said I didn't want to come," Chad responded.

Sonny took a deep breath. "Are we done here?"

Chad nodded curtly. "We are *beyond* done," he said, still staring at Sonny.

"Good," she said.

"Good," he answered.

And with that, they marched off in opposite directions, their heads held high. Sonny couldn't believe how arrogant Chad was acting. I'll show him, Sonny thought. She was going to throw the best prom *ever*!

That night, Nico and Grady showed up at the *So Random!* prop house dressed in tuxedos. They looked sharp, stylish, and definitely ready for a prom. As they straightened each other's ties, Nico said, "I'd say we clean up pretty nice." He patted down his suit and smiled.

"Why sir, you look . . . smashing," Grady remarked formally.

"As do you, sir, as do you," Nico replied jokingly, using a similar tone of voice.

Just then, Tawni entered the room wearing a beautiful long gown and a tiara.

Grady looked at her, impressed. "Wow, Tawni, you look really—"

She held up a hand. "Hold that obvious thought." She paused. "Okay, you are now free to ooh and aah," she said haughtily. She clicked a bejeweled music player that was clipped to her waist. Suddenly, the sound of trumpets blared out of the gadget.

But before Nico and Grady could respond, their attention was caught by something behind Tawni.

"Whoa," they said in unison.

Tawni smiled with satisfaction. "Also acceptable," she said, pleased with their response.

But Nico and Grady just pointed over her shoulder. Tawni turned to see Sonny walk in, dressed in a stunning long-sleeved dress. The boys smiled appreciatively.

"Oh, stop," Sonny said, blushing as she saw Nico and Grady looking at her with obvious approval. She took in the others' prom attire and smiled. "Look at us—we all look so prom-y," she said happily.

Just then, Zora walked into the room. She was dressed in black and wearing a headset. She looked very official. "Attention, prommers!" she shouted. "Marshall has left the building. Come on, let's make dreams happen! Go, go, go!" she ordered sternly. Quickly, she shooed the group out of the room.

As Nico and Grady left, Tawni turned to Sonny and gave her a questioning look. "You're not suddenly interested in being prom queen, right?" she asked accusingly.

"No," Sonny replied.

"Okay," Tawni said, relaxing a bit. "Then you look really pretty." She gave Sonny a small smile and rushed out of the room.

Left alone for a moment, Sonny spun around. "Look at me," she said to herself, delighted. "Twirling my way to the prom."

She continued to spin her way across the room, through the door—and right into Marshall, who was walking down the hall carrying his briefcase!

"Marshall!" she cried out in surprise. "You're not supposed to be here!"

He looked at Sonny disapprovingly. "And *you're* in a fancy dress," he pointed out. "*Twirling.* At seven o'clock at night." He looked stern. "In my office. Now."

He stalked into his office. Sonny reluctantly followed behind him. She had never seen

Marshall this angry before. She had a feeling her prom dreams were about to be shattered.

"Look at me, twirling my way into trouble," she muttered. This is not going to be good, Sonny thought, as the chance of her getting to dance at the prom was beginning to look slim.

CHAPTER 5

A few moments later, Sonny was sitting in Marshall's office, trying to look innocent.

"So you're here late, you're all dressed up, and I'm thinking all signs point to one thing," Marshall said and then paused. "You're doing a prom sketch."

Sonny let out a sigh of relief. "Yes!" she said eagerly. Maybe this would go better than she had thought!

"I like it! Let's have a little brainstorm. What

have you got so far?" Marshall asked.

"Um," Sonny said, trying to think fast. "Well, there's this girl. And she's dressed like this." She pointed to herself. "And she's late for the prom that she's waited her whole life for."

Marshall frowned. "Is this sketch going to get funny soon? Because it actually sounds kind of sad," he commented.

"Yes, trust me, I'm working on it," Sonny told him, trying to sound convincing.

Marshall looked at her curiously. Sonny tried to keep her composure. She knew she better come up with an idea, and fast!

Meanwhile, the "secret prom" was ready for action. The stage looked absolutely magical. It was decorated with balloons and twinkling lights, and packed with kids from the various TV shows that were filmed on the studio lot. Nico stood with three girls from the show *Meal or No Meal*,

31

who were all carrying lunch boxes with numbers on them.

Suddenly, Zora ran up to them, hysterical. "Red alert! Red alert! Marshall's back, and Sonny is stuck in his office!" she shouted.

"I thought it was your job to keep an eye on him," Nico told her.

Zora gave him an exasperated look. "It was! But he's like a jungle cat!" she replied.

Nico thought for a moment, then perked up. "Okay, I've got an idea that'll get him off the lot," he said, smiling.

Zora rubbed her hands together mischievously. "You get him off the lot, and I'll *keep* him off the lot," she said. Then she took out her cell phone and gave it to Nico. She sure hoped her plan would work!

Back in Marshall's office, Sonny was listening to Marshall ask question after question. ". . . So the prom's going on," Marshall was saying, "and this poor girl is still stuck in the office. She can hear the thump, thump, thump, of the music."

"Yeah, and just when the girl thought it couldn't get any worse, it did!" Sonny added, trying to remain patient.

At that moment, Marshall's phone rang. He hit the button for the speakerphone. "Hello?"

A voice boomed through the speaker. "Marshall Pike! This is Chip Dipper from K-HUG radio. Congratulations! You've won a valuable prize."

Sonny could tell that the voice belonged to Nico, but she hoped Marshall couldn't!

Marshall's eyes lit up. "I won a valuable prize!" he exclaimed.

"All you have to do is get in your car with your GPS *right now* and come down to the station to claim it," Nico went on.

"What's my valuable prize?" Marshall asked eagerly.

"Who cares?" Sonny exclaimed. She wasn't entirely sure what was going on, but if it got Marshall off the lot, that was good enough for her! "It's valuable! Go get it!" she encouraged him.

Marshall jumped up. He couldn't contain his excitement. "I'm leaving right now!" He quickly hung up the phone, practically shaking with anticipation. He grabbed his GPS. "I've only had this for a day, and it's already paying for itself!" he said joyfully to Sonny as he rushed out of the office.

Once she was alone, Sonny waited for a few moments to make sure the coast was clear.

"Finally, the part where the girl gets to go to her prom," she said, smiling to herself. Then she stood up and dashed off to do just that.

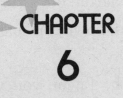

CHAPTER
6

Back at the prom, Tawni was standing next to a refreshment table piled high with food and soft drinks. Three very muscular guys walked over to her.

"Ooh, you must be the *Tweenage Gladiator* hunks," she cooed. "I'm Tawni. I'll be your prom queen for the evening. And as your prom queen, I'd just like to say—" Suddenly she stopped in midsentence, noticing that the trays of food were empty. "Hey! You ate all our food!" she yelled. But the boys were already gone. She picked up a couple of the empty trays and walked off.

As Tawni ran down the hall, Sonny raced toward her.

"Oh, my gosh, Tawni, you will not *believe* what just happened to me," Sonny gushed. "Marshall just caught me, and I got stuck in his office—" she rambled.

"We need more food!" Tawni exclaimed, cutting her off. She thrust the trays at Sonny. "Here."

"*Already?*" Sonny asked. "The prom just started!"

Tawni shrugged. "I know. Those gladiators are animals," she said, grimacing. Then she smiled at Sonny. "I can't wait to get back in there!"

Sonny's face fell. "Get back? I haven't even been in there once yet." Sonny let out a sigh.

This was not the way she imagined her prom night to be.

"Oh, it's fabulous," Tawni said brightly. "You've really outdone yourself."

Then she ran off, leaving Sonny to do all of the work. Again.

As Marshall jumped in his car, on his way to claim what he *thought* was a fantastic prize, he entered the address of the radio station into his GPS system. Little did he know that the address didn't even exist!

Back in Marshall's office, Zora was on the job. She sat at Marshall's desk, wearing a headset that was tapped into his GPS system. In a perfect imitation of the GPS's automated voice, she said, "Welcome. Is your seat belt fastened?"

"Yes," Marshall replied.

Zora continued talking in the GPS voice. "Please proceed point eight miles, and make a right," she said. "Then another left. Then a right. Then two more lefts. Then a left and a right and a left and a right and a left and a right."

As Marshall followed her very thorough directions, Zora put her feet up on the desk. "I was born for power," she said aloud to herself, smiling. Her plan, so far, was working perfectly!

CHAPTER
7

The prom was still in full swing, but Sonny wasn't able to enjoy it at all. Instead, she was rushing down the hall with a tray piled high with food.

"Pigs in a blanket coming through!" she yelled.

Suddenly, the heel on Sonny's shoe broke. She stumbled forward and the tray crashed to the ground. She looked around at the mess as everyone stared at her. She sighed. "I'm hoping the five-second rule applies here," she said glumly. Could anything else possibly go wrong? Sonny thought.

Just then, a group of kids who were rushing to get to the dance suddenly came in and trampled the hot dogs that were on the floor. Yup, Sonny thought. They certainly can.

Sonny stared after them as they pushed through the doors leading to the soundstage. "Hey, I still had three more seconds!" she yelled. She picked up her tray. Luckily, some of the pigs in a blanket were still on the tray.

Just then, Sonny looked up to see Chad standing in front of her.

"*Chad?*" Sonny asked in disbelief. "What are you doing here? You weren't invited!"

Chad looked at her and smiled cockily. "I was invited, but I didn't want to go. Then I was uninvited, so I knew I *had* to go," he replied, reaching out for one of the snacks on Sonny's tray.

"No, no, no!" Sonny shouted. "You're *not* going into my prom before I do! And these are for *invited* guests," she told him, pulling the tray of food away from him.

"So you're saying I can't have one?" Chad asked innocently.

"Yeah, you heard me!" Sonny said defiantly. She couldn't believe that he actually was crashing her prom!

Chad smirked. "Well, then I *have* to have one," he told her, grabbing a pig in a blanket off the tray.

"Hey!" Sonny cried.

"This tastes good," Chad said, chewing thoughtfully. "But you know where it would taste better? At the *prom*!" And with that, he headed inside.

Sonny was furious! "Hey, Chad, get back here!" she shouted. Just then, Grady and his dance partner came spinning out of the prom and smacked right into Sonny, accidentally tearing off one of the sleeves of her dress! The tray of food slipped out of her hands, again. And now her dress was destroyed.

"Ugh!" Sonny cried. "I have no food, and my dress is ruined!" Then she sighed. "But I'm still going to make this a night to remember." She looked down at her dress and frowned. "I can't go into the prom like this," she said sadly, her eyes welling with tears.

But then she straightened her shoulders and forced a smile. She walked out of the room and headed straight for the *So Random!* wardrobe department. She had an idea. She was *not* going to let her prom pass her by!

"There has got to be another dress in here *somewhere*!" Sonny cried. She rummaged through a pile of clothing. She suddenly spotted a queen costume. Hmm, I guess it's not ideal, but it's better than nothing, Sonny thought, quickly putting it on.

Just then Tawni walked into the room. She

gave Sonny a long, hard look. "Well, well, well," she said suspiciously. "I send you out for food, and you return with a knife for my back," she said, crossing her arms defiantly.

"What are you talking about?" Sonny asked in confusion.

Tawni rolled her eyes. "Isn't it *obvious*? You're dressed like a queen! You're trying to steal my crown. This is what you've been waiting your whole life for! This is why you moved here from Wisconsin!" she shouted.

Sonny looked at Tawni in disbelief. "What?" she asked. "Tawni, my dress was covered in food. I had to find something else to wear. It was either this or the mermaid outfit!" she exclaimed defensively.

Tawni gave Sonny a pointed look. Sonny rolled her eyes and threw the mermaid costume on over her dress. "Happy now?" she shouted back. Tawni smirked.

Sonny was determined to see at least a few minutes of the prom, even if she had to be dressed like a mermaid to do it. She quickly brushed past Tawni and headed out of the room.

Back in Marshall's office, Zora was still leading the *So Random!* producer on a wild-goose chase. "Now make a right," she directed in her GPS voice.

"That's my fourth right!" Marshall yelled, exasperated. "I've made a complete circle!" *That's it! Marshall thought. I'm getting rid of this GPS as soon as I claim my prize!*

Before Zora could continue, the office door opened. Nico stood there, holding up the torn sleeve of Sonny's prom dress. "Hey, Zora," he said. "Have you—?"

In the car, Marshall's eyes widened. *"Zora?!"* he asked.

Nico looked at Zora's headset in confusion. "Marshall?" he asked.

Now Marshall was frowning. "Chip Dipper?" he asked, thinking he was talking to the radio DJ. He was totally confused.

"No, it's Nico!" he exclaimed. Then he realized what he had just said. Oops, he thought. I probably shouldn't have said that!

"Nico?" Marshall asked in surprise. "What are you doing on my GPS? You kids are up to something. I'm coming right back," he said sternly.

Nico looked over at Zora apologetically. "That was probably the wrong thing to say," he told her. Zora just sighed. Her plan had worked, for a little while at least!

Just then, Sonny ran into the room completely out of breath.

"Sonny, we got a big problem," Zora told her in a serious tone.

"Really?" Sonny asked. "Is it worse than this?" she said, gesturing to her mermaid costume.

"It's about equal," Zora replied. "Marshall's coming!" she cried.

Sonny's jaw dropped. Could this day possibly get any worse?

CHAPTER
8

Sonny ran out of Marshall's office and headed straight for the room where the prom was being held. She burst onto the stage. "Kill the lights and pop the clouds!" she yelled into the microphone.

A murmur rippled through the crowd, and then people immediately started tearing down decorations, hoping to turn the prom back into a working soundstage before Marshall arrived.

Tawni, clutching her tiara, ran over to Sonny, who was yelling directions. "What about prom queen?" Tawni wailed. "We have to announce the prom queen!"

Sonny rolled her eyes, then grabbed the tiara and plopped it on Tawni's head. "Yay," she said sadly. "You're prom queen."

Tawni gasped and tears filled her eyes. "Me?! Really?" she cried. "This is *so* unexpected. Thank you so, so much."

But Sonny didn't have time to listen to the rest of Tawni's acceptance speech. She had to make sure Marshall didn't see any of this! She turned on her heel and rushed out the door just in time to intercept Marshall, who was heading straight for the soundstage doors. She joined him and jogged along at his side, trying to act casual.

"Marshall!" she said brightly. "You're back!"

He gave her a skeptical look. "Sonny . . . You're a fish," he said slowly.

Sonny bit her lip and tried to think of an explanation. They had almost reached the doors to the soundstage. "Yeah, if you're up for it, I would love to explain it anywhere else but here . . ." she began.

But it was too late. Marshall was already heading through the doors. "Or, we can do it here," Sonny said aloud to herself. She held her breath as she followed Marshall into the room. Inside, Nico, Grady, and Zora were standing on an empty stage, holding scripts. The only sign of a prom was the silver disco ball still hanging from the ceiling.

Marshall looked at his actors suspiciously. "So let me get this straight," he said, his brow furrowed in confusion. "You kids all sent me on a wild-goose chase so you could work on your sketch?"

"Sure!" Sonny said quickly. "Let's go with that."

Marshall shook his head in disbelief. "You know what?" he said, smiling a little. "You kids work too hard. Forget the prom sketch. Have yourself a real prom. Hey, you could do it in here!"

Sonny's jaw dropped. After all the work they had done to keep their prom a secret, *now* he was telling them that none of it had been necessary? "You have got to be kidding me," she said.

"I call prom queen!" Tawni exclaimed, before escorting Marshall out of the room.

"For what it's worth, you threw a cool prom, Sonny," Nico said, once Marshall was out of earshot.

Grady nodded. "Sorry you didn't get the chance to enjoy any of it."

As the two boys wandered away, Sonny slumped down in a chair. She was exhausted.

Suddenly, the lights dimmed. A spotlight hit the disco ball, and sparkling lights bounced around the room. Then the spotlight fell on Chad, who was standing alone in the middle of the floor.

"Hey," he said.

Sonny looked up wearily. "What are you still doing here?" she asked. "I thought you'd be the first to go."

He shrugged, half smiling. "Which is exactly why I had to be the *last* to go," he said.

"Well, you were right. All proms end in disaster," Sonny said, gesturing toward the empty stage.

His smile widened. "Do they, Sonny?" he asked. "Do they really?"

He pulled an electronic music player and headphones out of his pocket. He put one earphone in his ear and handed the other to Sonny. She put it in her ear and took the hand he held out for her.

As they began to slow dance, she said softly, "This is really sweet."

"I have my moments," he said, smiling at her.

"Are you going to press PLAY?" Sonny asked

a few seconds later. They had been dancing in silence.

"Oh. Right," Chad said, blushing slightly. "Sorry."

He pressed the PLAY button, and they started dancing again, this time to a fun, upbeat tune.

Sonny smiled. It wasn't necessarily the way she had imagined her prom . . . but, somehow, it felt exactly right.

PART
TWO

CHAPTER
1

Sonny Munroe had just finished rehearsing a skit on the hit sketch-comedy show, *So Random!* She was walking down the hall, taking off her blond wig, and recording a voice-mail greeting on her new cell phone. "Hi, this is Sonny, and you've reached me on my new cell phone at 555"—she pulled a piece of paper out of her pocket and read the rest of her phone number—"0125."

She clicked her phone shut and shook her head. "Way too perky," she muttered.

She let out a sigh and headed toward her dressing room. Just then, Josh, the guy who delivered the mail, pushed his cart out of her dressing room.

"Hey, Josh," she said, giving him a smile.

"Hey, Sonny, what's up?" he replied.

Before she could answer, Chad Dylan Cooper appeared behind Josh, carrying a script. Chad was the supercool, superfamous star of *Mackenzie Falls*, a top-rated tween drama series. He had been an actor for a long time—ever since he was a kid—and he usually didn't bother hanging out with other actors, let alone other actors from the show that was a *Mackenzie Falls* rival.

And yet, here he was.

"Hey . . ." he said casually to Sonny.

Sonny couldn't hide her surprise. "Chad!" she exclaimed. "What are you doing, and why are you doing it here at *So Random!*?"

He gave her a know-it-all look. "Because I'm not just the star of *Mackenzie Falls*, America's number one tween drama," he bragged. "I *also* got a part in a movie."

Sonny frowned slightly. "Still don't know why you're here," she commented.

"I'm playing a mail-delivery guy at a high-powered law firm," he explained. "It's a small but crucial role. So I'm following my good buddy Jeff around."

"It's Josh," Sonny said, correcting him.

Chad looked confused. "Who's Josh?"

Josh raised his hand. "That would be me."

Sonny turned back to Josh. "Well, good luck."

"Thank you," Chad replied.

Sonny raised an eyebrow. "I was talking to Josh," she said.

She walked away and headed into the dressing room that she shared with Tawni Hart. Her castmate was sitting in her favorite spot—in front of the mirror—and reading a letter from a pile of fan mail.

Sonny flipped open her cell phone to re-record her greeting in a less perky voice. "Hi, you've reached 555"—once again, she held up the piece of paper to remind herself what her number was—"0125. You know what to do."

She hung up. Seconds later, Sonny heard the sound of a cow mooing and her face lit up. "Hey, my first call!"

When she answered, she was surprised to hear Tawni's voice.

"Yeah, it's me," Tawni said from across the room. "Can you keep it down? I have twenty pounds of fan mail to go through."

Sonny hung up, then turned around in her chair to talk to Tawni. "Fan mail? Hey, did I get any?" she asked eagerly.

Tawni put her cell phone to her ear and held up one finger as if to say, "just a second."

Sonny's phone rang again. "Hello?" she answered.

"Oh, I was hoping to get your machine," Tawni said flatly. "Anyway, no fan mail for you." She hung up the phone again.

Sonny tried not to show how disappointed she was. "That's okay," she said with a shrug, trying to sound casual.

Tawni shot her a curious look. "I said you have *no* fan mail," she repeated.

Sonny nodded. "I heard you."

Tawni turned to look at Sonny more closely. "Doesn't that bother you?" she asked. "I mean, when I joined the show, my fan mail started arriving right away." Without letting Sonny see what she was doing, Tawni secretly dialed her cell phone again.

"It doesn't bother me," Sonny said calmly, just as her phone mooed again. She picked up. "Hello?"

"Does it bother you now?" Tawni said into her own phone.

Sonny closed her phone. "No," she said, but she was lying. It *was* really bothering her.

But I'm new to the show, Sonny thought. I'll get some fan mail soon. She decided to focus on more important things, such as rehearsing for another skit. She grabbed a baby bonnet and bottle, then headed for the door. "And now I'm off to rehearsal," she said. "Besides, I'm not going to let this bother me. I'm *way* too mature."

As Sonny headed out of the room, she breathed a sigh of relief. She hoped that Tawni wasn't on to her. She just wished that she would get some fan mail sooner rather than later!

Sonny walked onto the set wearing her costume, ready for rehearsal to start. Marshall Pike, the producer of *So Random!*, was eyeing a table piled high with food that the craft services department

Part 1

"I'm thinking we can have our own prom,"
Sonny told her castmates.

"I will be your prom queen!" Tawni announced.

Sonny couldn't wait for the prom!

Sonny was still in her producer Marshall's office—he wouldn't stop talking!

"Marshall's back and Sonny's stuck in his office," Zora said.

Zora and Nico had a plan. They hoped it would work!

The cast of *So Random!* was pretending to rehearse their prom sketch when Marshall walked in.

"Sometimes, you get to dance with that one special person..." Chad told Sonny.

Part 2

"I said you have no fan mail. Doesn't that bother you?" Tawni asked Sonny.

"No, we can't open that. It's Zora's!" Grady shouted.

Sonny read the fan letter she
had written to herself.

Sonny pretended to talk to her fake fan, Eric,
on the phone. This was *not* going well.

Tawni agreed to give "Eric" a tour of the set, not realizing that it was actually Sonny in disguise!

"Where's your visitor's pass?" Nico asked Eric.

"Those are all for me?" Sonny cried, when she discovered her hidden fan mail.

Sonny was shocked when Chad came out onstage dressed as Eric!

had put out for the cast and crew to snack on.

"Hey, Marshall," Sonny said.

"Hey, kiddo," he replied. "Great rehearsal. I love you in that 'Baby Wah-Wah' sketch."

"Thanks," she answered modestly.

"When you spit up on the changing table . . . I laughed so hard," he added.

Sonny was happy that he liked her sketch, but there was still something bothering her. She sighed. "Look, Marshall, do you think it's weird that I haven't gotten any fan mail yet?"

Though Marshall did think this was a little odd, considering how popular their show was and how much fan mail the other actors got, he couldn't tell Sonny that. "No, not at all. Not everybody gets fan mail," he said, trying to sound as sincere as possible.

Just then, Josh and Chad walked over. Josh was pushing his mail cart as Chad was taking notes.

"Here's your fan mail, Marshall," Josh said, handing over a stack of letters.

Chad wrote down what Josh had just said. After all, it was important for an actor to know everything about his character and how he would behave in real life. "Announce mail," he said aloud to himself, "then *present* mail."

Sonny looked at the producer in dismay. "*You* get fan mail?"

"No, no," Marshall said quickly. "It's not fan mail. I get letters from people I don't know . . . who admire me and—"

Sonny gave him an accusing look. "That would be fan mail," she said dejectedly.

"Well, if you want to put a label on it," he said, hoping to lighten the mood.

But Sonny didn't laugh. Marshall even gets fan mail! she thought. I guess becoming popular in Hollywood is harder than I thought. A *lot* harder.

CHAPTER
2

Grady Mitchell and Nico Harris, two other *So Random!* cast members, were trying to answer their own fan mail, but they were finding it hard to concentrate. They were sitting on a couch in the prop house, going through their letters. A tall box marked PRIVATE AND CONFIDENTIAL: DO NOT OPEN was sitting on a cart next to the couch, but they were doing their best to ignore it.

"Look at all this fan mail," Nico commented.

"I know," Grady said. "Are we the luckiest guys in the world or what?" He opened a letter and peeked inside.

"But none of it matters, because all I can think about is what's inside *that* box," Grady complained.

Nico looked at him. He and Grady were opposites in a lot of ways. For example, Nico thought of himself as smooth and charming, while Grady tended to bounce around like an overgrown puppy dog. But in other ways, they were very much alike. And right now, Nico was sure that he and Grady were thinking exactly the same thing about that box.

"Let's open it," Nico said eagerly.

Grady stood up, holding a manila envelope. "No, no, we can't do that," he protested. "It's Zora's, and it says 'Private and Confidential: Do Not Open.'"

Nico rolled his eyes. "Yeah," he replied, "but

if you stand like this . . ." He grabbed the envelope from Grady and leaned his arm over the box, covering every word but the word OPEN. He gestured toward the words, smiling. "It just says OPEN," he said.

Nico had a point, Grady thought. In fact, he had an *excellent* point.

But just as Grady reached for the box to peek inside, a plastic arrow flew through the air. The suction cup on the end of the arrow shaft stuck firmly to Grady's forehead.

He gasped and looked around to see where it had come from. Zora Lancaster was standing a few feet away, holding a toy bow and arrow. She had an angry look on her face.

"Back away from the box or it's going to get messy," she commanded.

"What's the big deal, Zora?" Nico asked. "We weren't *really* going to open it."

"Yeah, right," Zora scoffed. "You guys

open every package I get and eat what's inside. Whether or not it's food." Zora gave them both an exasperated look and then began wheeling her box out of the room.

But Grady couldn't stand the suspense. He was dying to know what was in that box!

"Come on," he pleaded. "What's inside the box?"

Zora paused and gave them a sly smile. "You really want to know?"

Nico and Grady exchanged surprised glances. "Yeah!" they cheered in unison. "Tell us!"

Zora's eyes glistened. "Okay, come real close," she said. "I'll tell you . . ."

As they leaned toward her, Zora's smile disappeared. "None of your business!" she yelled, right in their faces. She left the room, taking the box with her. "So keep your mitts off my mail, punks," she added.

Grady and Nico looked at each other slyly.

Maybe they wouldn't be able to find out what was in the box immediately, but they would eventually. When there's a will, there's a way! Grady thought mischievously.

CHAPTER 3

"**W**ah-*wah*-wah," Sonny said, staring into her dressing-room mirror. Her long brown hair was tucked up under a baby bonnet. She was sucking on a bottle and holding a script as she rehearsed.

She shook her head at her reflection. "That's not good." She tried again. "*Wah*-wah-wah."

Was that better . . . or worse? Sonny sighed. She'd been working on this skit for so long that she didn't know anymore.

Just then, Tawni breezed through the door

and gave Sonny a fake smile. "Still crying about no fan mail?" she asked haughtily.

"No. I told you, I'm *totally* fine with that," Sonny said, trying to sound nonchalant. She took off her bonnet. She was tired of rehearsing.

"Right," Tawni replied. "Maybe someday you'll get a fan letter like everyone else. Me, Zora, Grady, Nico, Marshall, *me*."

Sonny felt a wave of irritation sweep over her. She couldn't believe how self-centered Tawni was! And Sonny also couldn't believe that she was so unpopular that she hadn't gotten any fan letters *at all*!

Just then, Sonny spotted a menu from a Chinese restaurant on her desk. An idea popped into her head. She quickly picked up the menu and folded it so that it looked like a letter.

"For your information," Sonny began, "I *did* get a letter today, from . . ." She glanced at the menu. "Royalty. A *king*, no less!"

Tawni picked up another copy of the menu, which was on her desk. "Oh, really?" she said, scanning the front of it. "Could it be . . . the *Hunan King*? And does he live in a noodle palace?"

Sonny tried to bluff. "Actually, he has *seven* locations," she began. Then she gave up. "All right, fine, it's a menu! I didn't get any stupid fan mail."

"Sweetie, I know it must hurt to be so unpopular," Tawni said, her voice syrupy sweet. "Well, I don't *know*, I can only imagine. Just like you can only imagine what it's like to be popular. I mean, each fan letter is like a hug from a friend."

Sonny glared at her. "Is this pep talk almost over?" she asked.

"Well, let's see." Tawni pretended to give this some thought. *She* was certainly feeling better, even if Sonny wasn't. "*I* got more pep. So, yeah, all done!" She picked up a script and started to leave.

"I *have* fans, you know," Sonny insisted.

"Sure you do," Tawni cooed. "They just haven't had time to write yet." And with that, she walked out the door, grinning.

Sonny stared after her, seething. Then she noticed her pen, sitting right next to the note with her new cell-phone number written on it. Another idea popped into her head, an even *better* one.

"Dear Sonny . . ." she began to write. She wouldn't be the only cast member without fan mail for much longer!

CHAPTER 4

Nico and Grady were hovering over the craft-services table, staring hungrily at all the food.

"Dude," Grady said. "You see what I see?"

"Chocolate-covered, caramel-filled nut clusters," Nico replied happily.

Grady shook his head. "No, but grab me a few of those while I tell you the other thing," he said, pointing. "Over there. The forbidden box."

Sure enough, Zora's mysterious box was sitting on the floor a short distance away. Nico and Grady glanced around the soundstage.

"And no Zora," Nico pointed out.

"No Zora," Grady said, grinning. The coast was clear!

As Nico and Grady moved stealthily toward Zora's box, Sonny was focused on a secret mission of her own. She walked past Josh, who was still pushing his mail cart, and Chad, who was still monitoring Josh's every move. She looked around and sneakily slid an envelope onto the cart without being seen.

"Josh, come on," Chad whined. "I think I'm ready."

"But I don't," Josh replied firmly.

"I just want to push the cart," Chad insisted.

"It's *my* cart," Josh pointed out.

Sonny shook her head. What was Chad thinking, trying to take over Josh's job? The guy took his mail-delivery duties *very* seriously.

She headed toward Marshall and Tawni, who were each sitting in a director's chair and reviewing a script.

"Hey, guys," Sonny said as casually as possible. "Sorry I'm late. Did I miss anything?"

Before they could answer, Josh and Chad arrived with the mail. Josh, of course, was still pushing the cart.

"Hey! Mail's here!" Tawni cried with delight. She turned to Sonny and added dismissively, "This doesn't concern you."

But Josh was holding out a letter in Sonny's direction. "Uh, Sonny, here's a letter for you," he said.

"For *me*?" Sonny said, pretending to be both astonished and pleased.

"For *her*?" Tawni repeated, even more shocked.

"Hey, I told you you'd get a fan letter!" Marshall said enthusiastically as Sonny opened the envelope. "Way to go, kiddo. Read it out loud."

"No, no, I don't want to brag," Sonny said, trying to sound modest.

Then, after a few seconds, she decided the time for modesty was over. She started to read the note. " 'Dear Sonny,' " she began. " 'My name's Eric, and *So Random!* is my favorite show. I didn't think it could get any better, but then you joined the cast. I think you're awesome and talented. Please say hi to Nico, Zora, Grady, and Marshall.' "

Marshall beamed. "Hey, I got a shout-out!"

Tawni was frowning. "*I* didn't," she pointed out.

"How nice is that letter?" Marshall said slowly. "You know what?" he continued, jumping up suddenly. "We should call this kid!"

"Yes!" Sonny cheered, caught up in the excitement. Then she remembered that this plan could pose a slight problem. "What? *No!* Why?"

"Because he's your first fan . . ." Marshall explained with a smile. "This is a big deal! And how exciting would it be for him to get a call from you?"

Thinking quickly, Sonny turned to Marshall. "I would love to call my first fan . . . too bad we don't have his number," she said, her voice tinged with false disappointment.

"Sure we do," Marshall replied. He held up an orange scrap of paper. "He left it on this note." He gave Sonny a wide smile.

Sonny's eyes widened with horror as she realized that the note with her new cell phone number written on it had somehow gotten stuck to the fake fan letter. Oh, no! Sonny thought. This could mean disaster!

Marshall took out his phone and began to dial.

"Wait! You can't just call someone out of the blue like that," Sonny protested.

"Sure we can," Marshall said. "You were so down in the dumps. This is the perfect pick-me-up!"

"But I'm not down anymore," Sonny said quickly. "I'm out of the dumps." She gave him a big smile.

Marshall ignored her. "Shh, it's ringing."

Suddenly, they heard the sound of a cow mooing.

The producer looked around. "Is that a cow?" he asked, puzzled.

"Uh, yeah, and it's right behind you!" Sonny said hastily. "Gotta go!" And with that, she ran out and headed for her dressing room to answer her phone. She had a plan, and she hoped it would work!

CHAPTER 5

Grady and Nico still hadn't given up on their mission to find out what was in Zora's box. They struggled to push the mystery box down the hall.

"How did Zora move this thing?" Grady groaned. "It weighs a ton!"

"Quit your beefin'," Nico said, panting slightly.

Just then, Sonny ran past them, her cell phone still mooing from her dressing room.

"Well, quit your *mooin'*," Grady told Nico.

Sonny continued racing down the hall and into her dressing room. She quickly answered her cell phone in a low voice that she hoped sounded like a teenage boy.

"Yo, 'sup?" she answered. "It's Eric."

Marshall was delighted to have made contact with Sonny's fan. "Eric, this is Marshall Pike, executive producer of your favorite show, *So Random!*," he said brightly. "I've got somebody I want you to talk to." He glanced around, and his face quickly fell. "Where's Sonny? Sonny? Sonny?"

Sonny put her phone on her dressing table and raced back to the soundstage. As she ran down the hall, she jumped over Nico and Grady, who were slumped on the floor next to Zora's box.

When Sonny reached Marshall, she was holding a turkey leg she had managed to snatch off the craft-services table in the middle of her mad dash from her dressing room.

"Sorry, just went to get a snack," she explained breathlessly.

"Your fan's on the phone," Marshall said.

Sonny grabbed the phone and held it to her ear. "Hi, Eric!" she exclaimed. "How are you doing?"

She pretended to listen. "Oh, nothing. Just eating a turkey leg . . ."

"Hey, I've got a great idea," Marshall interrupted. "Let's invite him to the studio."

"What?" Sonny shrieked. "No!"

He smiled at her sweetly. "Aw, you're shy about your first fan," he said. "Give me the phone, I'll do it."

Sonny clutched the phone to her. "No! I'll do it," she said quickly.

She spoke into the phone. "So, Eric, listen, we wanted to invite you down to the set to meet me. . . ."

She paused as if listening to his reply, then made a big show of looking disappointed. "What's that? You can't come? *Two* broken arms?"

Marshall tried to grab the phone, but Sonny scooted out of his way.

"Tell him we'll come to him," the producer suggested.

"We can't go to him!" Sonny answered, panicked.

"Why not?" Marshall asked.

"Uh . . ." Sonny stared at him blankly, then spoke into the phone. "Why can't we come to you, Eric? Uh-huh . . . uh-huh . . ."

Marshall tapped his foot impatiently. "What's he saying?"

Sonny waved him off. She was stalling for time, hoping to come up with a good excuse for why they couldn't go visit her fake fan at his fake home, but nothing was coming to mind. "Uh-huh," she said again as she racked her brain. "Uh-huh . . ."

Marshall reached for the phone again. "Give me the phone," he said firmly.

Sonny turned her back. "Uh-huh," she said. Cornered, she made a split-second decision. "So you can come?" she asked.

She closed her eyes briefly, wondering how she was going to handle this situation. Then, before Marshall could grab the phone, she said in a rush, "Okay." And she hung up just as Marshall managed to snatch the phone out of her hands.

Sonny shook her head and said, "You know, I have a feeling that kid's not showing up." She glanced down at the floor, pretending to look sad.

Phew, Sonny thought. She had been hired as the newest cast member for *So Random!* for her acting skills . . . but she didn't think she'd have to use them *off* the set, too! She was exhausted! She was satisfied with her performance, but she hadn't bargained for how protective her executive producer could be of his actors.

"Well, if he doesn't, I'm going to call him every day until he does," Marshall vowed. "You're meeting your fan whether he likes it or not!"

Sonny gave Marshall a nervous smile. What had she gotten herself into?

CHAPTER
6

Sonny was definitely in a sticky situation, but she had another great plan. She just hoped her idea would work! *Can I pull off dressing as a guy?* Sonny wondered nervously. After she was ready transforming herself into "Eric," Sonny showed up at the door to Marshall's office as a shaggy-haired fifteen-year-old boy. She was wearing an oversize hooded sweatshirt and baggy pants and had a cast on each arm.

"You must be Eric," Marshall said, greeting

who he thought was Sonny's fan. "Wow, you weren't kidding about those broken arms, were you?"

Sonny scowled at him. "You think this is funny?" she snarled. "How about I come over there and break your arms and you see how funny it is?"

Marshall took a step back, a little scared. "You seem a little different from your letter," he said nervously.

Sonny saw this as her chance to escape. "Look, if you don't want me here, I'll just leave," she said, turning to go. "I don't see Sonny here, anyway. See you later."

"Wait, wait, wait," Marshall said hurriedly. "You came all the way down here to meet Sonny, and you're going to meet Sonny."

Sonny hesitated. What was she going to do now? Marshall was determined to make her meet herself!

"Well, make it snappy," she growled, hoping she could figure out what to do next. "I got places to go, people to see when I . . . get to those places."

Just then, Tawni rushed through the door. "Marshall, I need to talk to you," she said, not noticing that Marshall had company.

"Oh, Tawni, you're just in time," Marshall said in a welcoming voice. "This is Eric—he wrote that fan letter to Sonny."

Tawni looked at Eric with disapproval. "Oh, the one that didn't mention me?" she said, giving Eric an angry scowl.

"Yeah, that's the one," Marshall said, oblivious to Tawni's snideness. "Can you keep him company while I go find her?"

Sonny's heart raced nervously. This day was going from bad to worse!

"I don't really think she wants to," Sonny said quickly.

"Actually, I'd be delighted," said Tawni, giving Eric a very approving look. Gross! thought Sonny. "Any fan of Sonny's is a fan of mine, right?" Tawni said.

Sonny rolled her eyes. "Not necessarily," she muttered as Tawni led her out of the office. Oh boy, Sonny thought. It's *really* time to put my acting powers to the test!

A short time later, Tawni finished giving Eric a tour of the *So Random!* studio, ending in the prop house.

"Well, thanks for showing me around," Sonny said, relieved that she had survived the tour. "I have to go."

But Tawni wasn't letting Eric leave just yet. "You know, there's something that's been bugging me ever since you wrote that fan letter to Sonny," she said. "Why would you write a fan letter to *Sonny*?" she asked, frowning.

Sonny gave her a hard stare. "Because I like her."

This answer only seemed to confuse Tawni. "Why do you like her?"

Sonny couldn't take it anymore. "Why don't *you* like her?" she demanded angrily.

"How do you know I don't like her?" Tawni asked, startled.

"Uh . . ." Sonny thought fast. "Call it dude's intuition."

Tawni sighed. "It's not that I don't like her," she said. "It's just that she's a lot better than I thought she was going to be."

Sonny was so surprised that she forgot to use her deep Eric voice. "Really?" she asked. Then, in a lower voice, she went on, "I mean, really?" She couldn't believe what Tawni had just said!

"Yeah, but I'd never tell her that," Tawni revealed.

"Why?" Sonny was so interested in the way this conversation was going she almost forgot that she was pretending to be someone else. "You're not threatened by her, are you?"

Tawni's eyes flashed angrily. "Why would I be threatened by her?" she demanded. "I'm prettier, I'm funnier, and my hair has more volume."

Sonny's eyes narrowed when she heard this—especially since she thought her own hair looked pretty good. "That's because you use so much product," she said, totally forgetting that she was supposed to be a guy.

Tawni gave Eric an appreciative glance. "Ooh, I like a guy who knows about product," she cooed, moving a little closer.

Sonny gulped. "And *I* liked it better when you stayed over there," she said.

"What does your dude's intuition tell you now?" Tawni asked flirtatiously.

"Uh, that it's time to take these broken

wings and fly," Sonny said, running out the door.

"You'll be back," Tawni called after Eric. "They *always* come back," she smugly said aloud to herself.

CHAPTER
7

Eric's escape from the clutches of Tawni Hart had been close—*too* close! Sonny, still dressed as her fictional fan, raced down the hall, thankful that she had managed to get away. But she wasn't safe just yet. In fact, she was running so fast that she smashed right into Nico and Grady, who were still trying to move Zora's box.

"Whoa, watch where you're goin' . . ." Sonny growled in her Eric voice.

"Who are *you*?" Nico asked.

Instantly, Sonny went on the offensive. "Who are *you*?" she replied gruffly.

But Grady wasn't about to let a stranger come to the set of *So Random!* and get snippy with them! After all, *they* were the stars of the show! "Who are *you*?" he retorted.

Sonny met his eyes defiantly. "Who are you?" she asked again.

Grady sighed. This could go on forever! "I'm just going to break the ice here," he said. "I'm Grady."

Nico lightly punched him on the arm. "Don't be giving away your identity. We're in the middle of a crime here," he whispered.

Grady thought about that for a moment and turned back to Sonny. "The name's Darlington. Rusty Darlington. And you are?"

Sonny was still trying to sound tough. "What's it to you?"

Grady blinked, a little taken aback by the

question. "For the answer, I must defer to my brother"—he nodded toward Nico—"Jacob Darlington." Nico nodded and turned to Sonny.

"Uh, I've got a question for you, kid," Nico said curiously. "Where's your visitor's pass?"

"I don't know," Sonny said. "Why are you lugging around a box that says, 'Property of Zora's'?"

Grady and Nico looked at each other nervously.

"And we accept that answer as your visitor's pass," Grady said. "Go on."

"Enjoy your visit to *So Random!*," Nico added.

Sonny raced down the hall. Another close call avoided! she thought.

"Okay, I'm going to show you one more time," Josh said. He and Chad were standing in the hall next to the mail cart. Josh stamped a piece of mail with the day's date, then handed the stamp to Chad.

Chad stamped another letter, mimicking Josh's action exactly.

But Josh just shook his head sadly. Chad still wasn't getting the hang of Josh's job. "I give up," he said.

Chad glared at Josh. He'd been stamping mail for an hour and his stamping hand was getting tired. "What was wrong with that one?" Chad asked.

"Everything," Josh complained.

Before Chad could protest, Sonny—still dressed as Eric—rounded the corner and ran right into him.

"Sorry," she muttered.

For just a moment, she and Chad looked into each other's eyes.

"Do I know you?" Chad asked.

She shook her head quickly. "Nobody knows me," she said. "Nobody will ever know me!"

Then she kept on speed-walking down the hall, trying not to break into a run. She had to get off the set—and fast!

CHAPTER
8

Finally, Sonny reached the sanctuary of her dressing room. She closed the door behind her and leaned against it, breathing a large sigh of relief.

Then a voice suddenly spoke. Oh, no, Sonny thought, not again!

"I knew you'd be back," Tawni said sweetly. She pulled back the curtains to her dressing area. "They always come back."

She smiled at Sonny and clapped her hands

twice. Instantly, all the lights dimmed except for one spotlight, which was focused on a revolving disco ball. The ball began to twirl, sending sparkling lights around the room while soft music poured out of hidden speakers.

"Now, where were we?" Tawni purred.

And then, rescue arrived in the form of Josh. "Mail call!" he yelled as he opened the door, accidentally pushing Sonny forward. One of the fake casts on her arm started to fall off, but she quickly shoved it back into place as Josh entered the room.

"Sorry, Tawni," he said when he saw Eric. "I didn't know you were entertaining."

"I'm always entertaining," Tawni snapped. Irritated, she clapped her hands twice again. The lights came back on, and the music stopped. "What do you want, Josh?"

He held up a stack of letters. "I have some fan mail for Sonny. Will you make sure she gets it?"

Tawni smirked. "Don't I always?"

She took the mail from him. As Josh left, Tawni pulled off the back cushion of the dressing-room sofa, stuffed the letters inside, and then replaced the cushion.

"Those are all for me!" Sonny cried, dropping her Eric voice.

"No, they're all for—" Tawni began, not realizing that Sonny's voice had changed.

Sonny took off her fake moustache and threw the casts off her arms.

"Sonny?!" Tawni exclaimed, shocked.

Sonny strode over to the sofa and started pulling out letters from behind the cushion. "You're hiding my fan mail?!" she shouted.

But Tawni was still focused on her own surprise. "You're pretending to be your own fan?!"

Sonny pointed an accusing finger at Tawni. "You committed mail fraud!" she yelled.

"*You* committed fan fraud!" Tawni shouted back.

"Fan fraud's not illegal!" Sonny pointed out.

"Mail fraud's not embarrassing!" Tawni responded.

Sonny smiled. "I'm not embarrassed, but apparently I'm better than you thought I'd be," she said in a taunting voice.

Tawni gasped. "I told that to Eric in confidence."

"Yeah, well, one thing about Eric . . ." Sonny said. "He's bad at keeping secrets."

Suddenly, there was a knock on the door.

"Knock, knock," Marshall called out. "It's Marshall. Can I come in?"

Tawni saw her chance for revenge. "Guess who else can't keep a secret?" she said to Sonny. Then she raised her voice. "Come on in, Marshall!"

As the producer entered the dressing area, Sonny slipped behind the curtain.

"Have you seen Sonny?" Marshall asked. "I can't find her anywhere."

Tawni grinned triumphantly. "You can't find her because—"

"Because I'm right here," Sonny said as she pulled back the curtain. She was once more dressed as her real self. All traces of Eric had vanished.

"No, you're not!" Tawni cried. "You're Eric!" She turned to Marshall. "She's Eric."

"No, I'm Sonny," Sonny said very slowly. She pointed to the producer and continued speaking as if to a very small child. "That's Marshall. And you're Tawni, remember?"

"Marshall, she's Eric," Tawni insisted. "She put on a costume, broke her arms, and pretended to be Eric."

Marshall looked back and forth from one girl to the other and grinned. "I see what's going on here."

Tawni threw up her hands. "Finally!"

He wagged his finger at Tawni. "Somebody's a little jealous about somebody's first fan," he said.

Sonny burst out laughing. Tawni glared at her.

"Fine," Tawni sniffed. "Well, let's see who gets the last laugh. Marshall, I say we track down Eric, bring him back here and introduce him to Sonny onstage, during the show, in front of the whole world. What do you think of that?"

Sonny stepped forward. "I don't like that idea," she said firmly.

"*I* like that idea," Tawni said.

Marshall's eyes were gleaming. "I *love* that idea," he said. "I'm going to go call him right now." He headed out of the dressing room.

A second after he left the room, Sonny's cell phone mooed.

Sonny and Tawni instantly looked at each other, with the same thought in their minds. Who was going to get to that phone first?

They both bolted for the table. Tawni beat Sonny by a split second. She grabbed the phone and held it up in Sonny's face, while backing toward the sofa.

"Ha-ha!" she said, taunting Sonny.

But before she could answer, Sonny picked up a cushion and threw it at Tawni. The phone was knocked out of Tawni's hand, and it flew through the air, emitting a long, slow "moooooo."

It landed on the floor in front of Tawni's dressing table. Both girls lunged for it again. Sonny landed on the ground and began crawling toward the phone on her elbows. She was . . . almost . . . there . . . but then Tawni grabbed her ankles and pulled her back.

When the phone mooed again, Tawni pinned down Sonny, sat on her back, and calmly picked up the phone and flipped it open.

"Yo, 'sup?" she said, imitating Eric. "You want me to meet Sonny in front of a live audience?"

She grinned. "They'd have to break my legs to keep me away," she said cheerfully.

She hung up and handed Sonny the phone. Sonny took her phone and immediately dialed a number. Seconds later, Tawni's phone rang.

Tawni answered. "Hello?"

"Will you get *off* me?!" Sonny yelled. Tawni stood up and gave Sonny a satisfied look.

Wow! Sonny thought. I had no idea being an actress would be so difficult. Talk about drama on *and* off the set!

CHAPTER 9

Later that night, the *So Random!* cast had just finished performing in front of an enthusiastic live audience.

"So long, everybody!" Sonny called out.

The audience applauded wildly as Sonny, Tawni, Nico, Grady, and Zora rushed offstage.

"Great show, everybody," Marshall said, beaming at them. "We're back for the sign-off in two minutes."

Sonny felt her heart race. This was it! She ran

over to the spot where she had stashed her Eric costume and began putting it on.

She was in such a rush, she didn't even notice Chad approach her from backstage.

"I knew I recognized you," he said slowly. He now realized why Eric had looked so familiar. It was actually Sonny in disguise!

Sonny sighed. It had been a very long week. She began to explain. In some ways, she thought, it might be a relief to get the truth out. "I sent myself a fan letter and then pretended to be my own fan," she admitted. "And now I'm supposed to go out onstage and meet the fan I was pretending to be." Sonny hung her head in embarrassment.

Chad took a moment to think, and then asked, "Why would you write yourself a fan letter?"

Sonny hesitated. "Because I lost faith in myself," she finally said.

Chad nodded, suddenly understanding. "Ah,

a classic case of actor's insecurity," he said, his voice warm and sympathetic. "You started doubting your abilities, wondering if you were good enough and if you deserved to be on TV."

Sonny stared at him in disbelief. "So you've been through this?" She couldn't believe what she was hearing. Chad Dylan Cooper *understood* her?

Chad gave her an incredulous look. "No," he said, as if that should be obvious. Then he grinned. "But I just made you *think* I had. Which is why I'll never have to go through this."

Sonny's jaw dropped. "You are unbelievable!" she exclaimed. "I *knew* it. You don't care! I thought we were having a real moment here."

At that moment, they heard Marshall's voice. "And now, please welcome back to the stage, the cast of *So Random!*"

Sonny looked at Chad. "That's my cue," she snapped.

"So what are you going to do?" he asked.

"You don't care, remember?" she said. "But I do! Excuse me, I have to go out there and embarrass myself."

She tossed the Eric costume on a chair and walked toward the stage. She joined her castmates in front of the curtain as the audience cheered.

"That's our show, everybody!" Marshall shouted into the microphone. "But before we say good night, we want to introduce you to a very special guest. The guy who wrote Sonny her very first fan letter . . . Give it up for Eric!"

"Eric, come out, come out, wherever you're not," Tawni said in a singsongy voice, looking directly at Sonny.

Sonny took a deep breath. It was time to admit the truth.

"All right, let's get this over with," she said, with a sigh. "Marshall, I have to say something."

Marshall looked a little puzzled at Sonny's serious tone of voice, but he handed the microphone to her.

She looked out at the audience and began: "Eric is—"

"Your biggest fan!" a teen boy's voice called out. Suddenly, Chad, dressed as Eric, stepped onto the stage next to Sonny.

The audience applauded wildly.

Tawni's jaw dropped. "That's impossible!" she cried. "Eric is not real!"

"But I'm standing right here," Chad pointed out, grinning. He turned to the audience. "Give it up for Sonny!"

The crowd cheered even louder.

"Why are you helping me?" Sonny asked Chad under her breath as the crowd cheered.

"I'm not helping you," he said, talking through his teeth as he smiled at the audience. "I just wanted to try on the beard."

She smiled at him. "Somebody cares."

Chad returned her smile. The cast continued to wave good night to the studio audience until the curtain finally dropped. And that's a wrap, Sonny thought happily.

The show had ended fifteen minutes earlier, but Nico and Grady still hadn't left the soundstage. They were in the prop house with Zora's box. Nico was using a crowbar to pry it open. As the sides of the wooden box fell away, the boys saw a smaller box, wrapped like a birthday present complete with a bow, inside.

"We're going to need scissors," Grady said.

Nico shook his head. "We don't need scissors," he said. "We just have to pull the bow."

More than a half-hour later, Nico was still struggling with the bow, which was now a tangled mess.

Grady stood by, holding a pair of scissors

ready. "May I?" he asked patiently.

"Stupid ribbon," Nico said, glaring at it.

But he stepped aside to let Grady cut through the knotted ribbon.

"Smell that?" Grady asked, sniffing the air.

"Mmm," Nico said, a blissful smile appearing on his face. "Smells like her grandma's homemade chocolate-chip cookies."

He and Grady both licked their lips. Zora's grandmother's cookies were legendary on the *So Random!* set. In fact, Nico and Grady could already taste them. . . .

They lifted the lid—and saw Zora's head sitting on a silver platter, surrounded by cookies!

She grinned. "Who wants a cookie?" she asked.

After a short, shocked silence, Nico and Grady screamed and ran out of the room.

Zora grinned to herself. She was an expert at

magic tricks, and her latest one had turned out wonderfully.

"Works every time," she said as she leaned over to take a bite of one very tasty chocolate-chip cookie.

Hollywood is calling!
Look for the next book in the
Sonny With A Chance series.

STAR POWER

Adapted by Lara Bergen

Based on the series created by Steve Marmel

Based on the episode, "Fast Friends," Written by Michael Feldman & Steve Marmel

It was lunchtime for the cast and crew of *So Random!*, the number one sketch-comedy show on TV. And it was Monday—which meant one thing: meatball sandwiches for everyone! As usual, Grady Mitchell and Nico Harris, the two male cast members of *So Random!* were very excited about this. They had very hearty appetites, especially when it came to meatballs.

"These are the greatest sandwiches *ever*," Nico said, reaching for another. He and Grady had brought a whole tray of them back from the cafeteria to enjoy in the privacy of the prop house, the group's favorite room to hang out in.

"I *love* Meatball Monday!" agreed Grady. He took a giant bite. Tomato sauce splattered everywhere. But Grady just shrugged and continued eating.

Just then, Tawni Hart, the longest-running cast member—and self-proclaimed "star"—of their show walked in. She took one look at Grady and shook her head.

"Here's a little Tawni tip for you," she told him, eyeing Grady's mess. "It's even tastier if some of it lands in your mouth."

Grady crossed his eyes in order to better see the tip of his nose, which was covered in sauce. "Yeah, well, I'm saving this for later," he told Tawni.

"I'd like to see *you* eat one of these sandwiches and stay clean," Nico added.

Tawni just rolled her eyes—again. Did she have to teach other people *everything*?

"It's easy," she said, "if you use Tawni Hart's patented 'bite, wipe, and gloss.'" She picked a sandwich up off the tray and, with her pinkies in the air, brought it carefully and slowly to her mouth. "Bite . . ." she said, taking a dainty nibble. "Wipe . . ." She took a napkin and dabbed at the tiniest drop of sauce. Satisfied, she crumpled the napkin and carelessly tossed it away. "And gloss! Okay, now you try," she said.

Nico and Grady looked at each other. "Bite . . ." they repeated, digging in obediently as sauce dripped out of their sandwiches. "Wipe . . ." Grinning, they smeared the sauce across their mouths with their sleeves. "And sauce!" they finished.

Tawni put her head in her hands. They

were hopeless. And utterly gross!

Just then, Sonny Munroe walked in, dressed up *way* more than usual. The group looked at her curiously. They were still getting to know their new castmate. She'd just moved to Hollywood from her hometown in Wisconsin and joined the show. The whole TV-star thing was new to her still—and sometimes it was even scary. But it was also a dream come true, and a challenge she was definitely up to.

"Hey, guys," Sonny said, giving a little twirl.

"Have a seat," mumbled Nico through a mouthful of food. "Meatball Monday!"

Sonny looked down at the plate of sloppy sandwiches and shook her head. "I'd love to, but I can't," she said with a grin. She smoothed her hair and waited for her castmates to ask her why it looked so styled and perfect . . . and why she wasn't wearing the jeans and comfy T-shirts she usually wore.

And she waited and waited. . . .

"Aren't you going to ask me why I can't get meatballs all over this really cute outfit?" Sonny asked impatiently. "That you've never seen before? That I'm *clearly* wearing for a reason?"

When no one responded, it became evident to Sonny that she'd have to take matters into her own hands.

"Okay, get off my back. I'll tell you," she said finally. "You know that entertainment show, *Tween Weekly TV*?"

Grady finally looked up from his sandwich. "Hosted by"—he wiggled his eyebrows and suavely lowered his voice—"Santiago Geraldo?" he asked, imitating the popular host.

Sonny beamed. "Exactly! They're doing a feature on me!" She clapped her hands and let out a squeal of delight. She could still hardly believe it. *Tween Weekly TV* was big-time!

Nico gave a nod of approval. "*Very* cool, Sonny," he said.

Tawni, meanwhile, dabbed at her mouth with a napkin and frowned. "Let me guess," she said to Sonny, "it's one of those, 'let's follow the new girl around' stories?"

Sonny nodded. "It is!" she exclaimed.

Been there, done that, Tawni thought. She sighed and put down her sandwich. "Which brings us to Tawni tip number two." She wagged a warning finger at Sonny. "Watch what you say, because you don't want to look bad on camera."

Sonny gave her a curious look. She was already used to Tawni's know-it-all attitude. And Sonny had to admit that because Tawni had been on TV since, well, preschool, she *did* know a lot about show business. But Sonny also knew that Tawni still wasn't happy about having a new girl on the show. Tawni didn't like sharing the spotlight— not at all!

"I'll be fine," Sonny assured her.

Tawni shrugged and went back to her lunch. Just then, Sonny heard her stomach grumble.

"You sure you don't want some?" asked Grady.

"Well, maybe just one little bite," Sonny said. A girl has to eat, she thought. She sat down, picked up a sandwich, and took a big bite. *Mmm . . .* That was good, she thought. *And* messy. She looked around for an extra napkin . . . just as Santiago Geraldo walked in, along with his camera crew.

Sonny didn't need a mirror to know her face was covered with tomato sauce, and Santiago Geraldo didn't need a director to tell him to have his cameraman start rolling.

"One girl. One meatball," said the gossip-show host. He held his microphone in front of Sonny's red face. "One quick thought?" he asked her.

Sonny waved as she tried to chew—and smile. "Hi, Mom," she mumbled, and blushed.

Santiago smiled broadly. "Reporting for *Tween Weekly TV*, I'm Santiago Geraldo." He wiggled his eyebrows in his trademark style, as Grady had done earlier. Sonny smiled sheepishly. Well, that wasn't exactly the first impression she had planned on giving!